'Climbing Mountains, Reaching Goals'

Author: Bernd Hans-Joachim Harry Braeuer

eBook ISBN: 979-8-89795-239-7
Paperback ISBN: 979-8-89795-240-3
Hardcover ISBN: 979-8-89795-241-0
Bernd Hans-Joachim Harry Braeuer-Luminari Books

Dedication

This book is dedicated to my son Jay and my good friend Gerry, who have both shown tremendous courage in their individual journeys of recovery from Acquired Brain Injury (ABI). The individual journey that my role played in their recovery has turned into an incredibly new and rewarding life path for me that continues to expand in meaning with each successive year.

Prologue:

In mid-1997, Bernd (Ben) Braeuer confronted a situation that no parent should ever have to experience. A phone call saw him rushing into the Gold Coast Hospital to be confronted with the sight of his youngest son barely clinging to life after a heart stoppage of over 25 minutes. What followed was a week spent with Jay in intensive care and a further month in hospital, the whole time by his son's side. As it happened, there was no service that could cover the different needs of Jay's ABI. So, Ben decided to set everything in his own life aside to manage his son's long-term recovery process full-time, no matter what it would take. This proved to be a supreme test of Ben's coping ability, with many challenges, unexpectedly also opening a path into a completely new life for Ben at the same time. An incredible journey followed that propelled Ben to study brain injury recovery, natural healing philosophies, Tai Chi, yoga, and Oriental and Native American cultural concepts and values. Ben soon found himself teaching yoga to private groups, conducting personal training for friends, then moving on to conduct a Self-awareness Program for local non-profit organisation Headway, assisting clients with recovery from Acquired Brain Injury (ABI), all whilst managing Jay's recovery. He drew in all of the specific services and support systems required to aid his healing process over the following 11 years.

This book covers Ben's time spent assisting Headway's clients on their ABI recovery journey, which led him to create 'Climbing Mountains, Reaching Goals'.

'Climbing Mountains, Reaching Goals' provides a simple and practical guide to overcoming the challenges we face in life. How to overcome the challenges despite the voices that echo, 'You'll never do that' … and to allow each of us to move forward toward achieving our Life Goals, no matter how lofty they might be.

Footnote: 'Climbing Mountains – Reaching Goals' also became an important unit of learning for disadvantaged and at-risk children participating in Youth Self-esteem and Leadership Programs and Camps developed for, and conducted over the past two decades by, Ben's Youth Charity - New Beginnings International.

Climbing Mountains, Reaching Goals – How the Program came to be:

<u>For the Love of a Son:</u>

It was one of those terrible moments when you feel suspended in time and space, totally helpless and beyond control. I had been idly pondering work papers at the desk in my bedroom alcove whilst speculating how much longer it would be before I could hear Jay opening the front door of our Parkwood home.

It was Tuesday, July 8th. Only a couple of hours ago, my son's voice on the answering machine had reassuringly said, "I'll be home at 6:30 pm at the latest!" It was his first day back at home after the term holidays. He had only just days ago moved back after living away from home for about 6 weeks. A time that had seemed the longest weeks of my life as it had been spent with not the best of companions. Understandably, I was slowly beginning to feel concerned.

At almost 7 pm, the phone rang.

"Is this Jay's father?" "Yes!" "Your son has just been admitted to the Gold Coast Hospital in critical condition."

What followed was a complete blur. I grabbed my mobile phone and wallet. As I rushed to slip into my shoes at the front door, I snapped at his older brother, "Jay's in hospital in Emergency. I'll ring you from the hospital as soon as I know more."

In the car, my mind raced over and over, picturing scenarios of what possibly could have happened. The morning's conversation replayed in my head, "Jay, I've got an appointment this afternoon." "Dad, I'm 17, I can look after myself. I'll take the bus home!". I said, "OK, Jay." As always, I felt caught up between the pressures of being both sole parent and family provider.

What followed were the hardest two months of my life, followed by another eleven difficult years. Our family had experienced trauma before, but nothing like this! As I learned from those who had come to Jay's aid, my son's heart had been stopped for over 25 minutes. What followed turned out to be both our worst nightmare that presented us with numerous challenges, but also a miracle that changed our lives for the better.

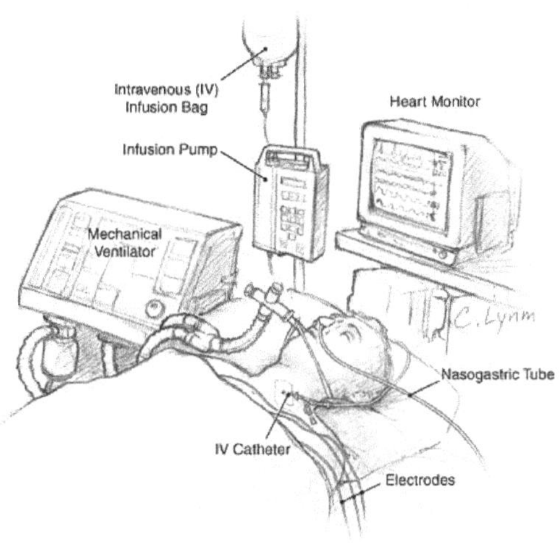

Drawing credit to the original artist

<u>Ben the Motivator</u>:

I guess I've always been a motivator, right from the early days of my 20-plus years on the international corporate scene working at the highest level with global giant firms Ericsson and, later, Siemens. So, it was not unusual to find myself being asked to run a Self-awareness group at Headway Gold Coast [1] during the management of my youngest son's recovery from an Acquired Brain Injury (ABI).

What is not well understood is that every ABI is different in nature, with treatments and support required in each case often radically different for a path to recovery. In the months following Jay's release after a month in the Gold Coast Hospital's general ward and another month of occupational therapy, I was faced with the question, "What's next?" Whilst Jay was still in intensive care, I asked one of the senior nurses to provide me with documents I could study on Acquired Brain Injury. That's always been my way. When confronted with a challenging situation, I would always throw myself into intense study to prepare myself to meet that new challenge. Soon, I was contacting and arranging appointments with different services for Jay, as well as arranging a variety of practical activities that would aid his recovery. This journey proved both complicated and rewarding at the same time. Halfway along the complex path of Jay's recovery, I connected with local Gold Coast service Headway. An organisation supporting clients recovering from ABI that would provide the next logical step for Jay's recovery by offering him one-on-one counselling support.

<u>The Challenge – Restoring the Self-worth of Headway's ABI Clients</u>:

Some years before my involvement with Headway, I had already developed my own motivational program, 'Focus for Achievement,' run for adult classes at Gold Coast TAFE and for one of the two Australian Americas Cup Yachting teams, Sydney 95, whilst they were training on Australia's Gold Coast in advance of the 2015 Americas Cup in San Diego.

So, I did not hesitate to take on this new challenge when Headway's Gold Coast manager, aware of my background, asked if I would be willing to run Self Awareness Group sessions for their clients. My brief was to help a group of Headway's ABI clients regain perspective and stability in their severely disrupted lives. I was only too pleased to give something back as a counter for the support Headway was providing for Jay!

The initial self-awareness group sessions were run in a large utility shed at the back of Headway's Southport premises. The group of clients was very diverse, some with very distinct ABI symptoms, others with what is known in the field of ABI recovery as an 'invisible disability,' showing little in the way of outward symptoms. Right from the start, I felt positive about being able to help Headway clients progress in their recovery.

<u>Gerry and the Group's Journey - Climbing Mountains, Reaching Goals' takes Shape</u>:

Several months before he joined my Self Awareness group, I remember noticing Gerry at Australia Fair Shopping

Centre. He stood out as he was being pushed along in his wheelchair by a young woman who I assumed to be his carer. I learned later that the woman was his dedicated partner, Julie.

On the day he was to join my Self Awareness group, Headway's Manager took me aside and explained that Gerry had been operated on for a brain tumour, and, as a result, had been significantly incapacitated. She suggested that I gently phase him into my self-awareness program. I soon learned from his partner that Gerry's brain surgeon had advised that 'Gerry will never walk or talk again,' or words to that effect following his surgery. It was to cast an immediate shadow over Gerry's life.

However, from the minute Gerry joined our group, I could sense something special about the way he was tuning in and responding. To illustrate my words and concepts to the group, I had spontaneously begun to draw freely with marker pens on the only thing immediately handy to me in Headway's back shed - large broken pieces of dusky pink Laminex. For this, I drew significantly on my own life experience and my 'Focus for Achievement' program.

I knew I had to motivate the group members to step out of their individual situations, to find something special within themselves, and to encourage them to take positive steps forward in their lives once again. Some of those referred to my Self-awareness group had acquired their ABI through car/motorbike accidents, others because of medical conditions. Just as Gerry had been told by his specialist that he would never walk or talk again, many thought they had little or no hope of recovery from their ABI.

So, my first sessions focussed on 'Stepping out of the Box,' something that their physician, others, or they had placed themselves in. I spontaneously came up with the analogy of 'Climbing Mountains' to address the challenges and setbacks they would face along the way to reaching their life goals. I spontaneously drew pictures of the different stages of the 'Mountain Challenge' recovery path I came up with on those discarded Laminex pieces.

Brain injury's not the end for Gerry

By VALERIE JONES

ASK Gerry Dyst his goal in life and he tells you, without a moment's hesitation, 'to live on my houseboat again'.

You have to really concentrate to hear Gerry describe his dream because he has acquired brain injury (ABA) from a brain tumour operation in September 1998, and speaking is a laborious and frustrating process for him.

Even just a few months ago Gerry's dream would have seemed to be of the 'impossible' variety, thanks to the terrible legacy of the operation which left him unaffected mentally but severely physically disabled.

But lately he's been making such good progress in his fight to live a 'normal' life, that those who know Gerry now see that his dream could very well, one day, become a reality.

Gerry, now 39, and the father of a boisterous two-year-old, was lucky to survive his operation which left him unconscious in intensive care for two weeks.

The previously super-fit dogman and scaffolder who had built his 54 foot house boat himself, recovered but with the legacy of horrendously debilitating ataxia (brain

SMOOTHER SAILING ... Gerry Dyst with wife Julie, son Jasper and meditation teacher Ben Brauer.

Everyone responded in one way or another, but Gerry seemed to internalise my lessons much more. Having gradually come to know more about him and his specific situation, I gave him a mantra to take away after one of the sessions:

'Every day, in every way, I'm getting better and better' [2].

- something that I had first come across in one of Peter Sellers 'Pink Panther' Films, learning later that it is well-known and used freely in psychiatric circles.

Gerry told us proudly at our next group session that he had been repeating that mantra to himself over and over again every single day. Shortly afterward, Gerry's partner Julie told our group that Gerry had entered the Masters Games, sailing a disabled dinghy. In our group session the week after his Masters Games event, Gerry very proudly produced the Bronze Medal he had won, to everyone's amazement.

I'm reminded of one other very memorable group session in that old shed behind the Headway office when I used meditation to provide a calm space for the group members. This time, I had chosen a song from a Native American album. The song was the well-known hymn 'Amazing Grace,' which is also the Cherokee national anthem, but sung in Cherokee, with bagpipe backing. I observed that every single person in the group was visibly moved. Some had tears in their eyes, and I could see some of the pain inflicted on them resulting from their disability begin to melt away – it was a magical moment in time! I also began to spend time individually with other group members, focussing on their specific, often complex recovery needs, always keeping in mind that my job was to motivate them.

Gerry continued to progress in his recovery, as did other members of the group in their own recovery journeys. Many realised that their constraints were artificial and could be overcome.

As a member of Southport Yacht Club and Chairman of Youth Sailing in that year, I often spent time at the club's Hollywell facility, where disabled sailing was being held weekly. I was present when Gerry was taking part in a sailing race with particularly strong and gusty wind conditions. Part-way through the race, the boom that was holding the foot (bottom edge) of the mainsail on his dinghy dislodged from the mast. Showing his determination, here was Gerry, still sailing, with one hand holding the boom in place and the other perfectly controlling the boat's tiller (steering) to finish the race. Way to go, Gerry!

I continued running my Self-awareness group sessions at Headway for some time, deepening the 'Climbing Mountains' concept each time, as well as introducing other relevant elements to try and lift the clients out of the 'boxes' they had been placed in. Sensing their need for 'time-out', I also took the group on frequent day excursions to locations in the Gold Coast's Hinterland in Headway's Minibus. Nature is a Healer. They all loved it.

On one other occasion with Gerry, I decided to try a one-on-one deep healing meditation with Gerry at his home. I applied the Native American healing practices that I had been taught by my good friend, a Native American Elder, Tony White Wolf. At the end of this very deep healing meditation, Gerry announced that he had begun to feel the nerve endings in his arms come to life for the first time since his brain injury during the session. A further breakthrough in his recovery!

<u>Gerry the Motivator - Reaching His Goal and much more</u>:

Gerry and his partner Julie had learned that I had begun running Self-esteem and Leadership Camps for disadvantaged and at-risk children as part of the youth charity I founded in 1999. Without hesitation, they both volunteered to assist, with Julie very capably running our camp facility's kitchen. Gerry soon became our chief motivator, impressing kids with the way he would scoot around the camp on his bottom (his legs not yet supporting his weight fully). Also, during our life stories presentation proudly showing off the three medals (one silver and two bronze) that he had since won in disabled sailing. The children at each of our camps never failed to be motivated by Gerry's drive to improve and his achievements. Based on the lessons I had taught at Headway, I had also included a learning module, 'Climbing Mountains, Reaching Goals,' into our Youth Camp program.

After my time with Headway came to its natural end, Gerry kept on progressing forward. He has been regularly bench pressing 180 Kilograms 200 times and has persisted in repeating the mantra I had given him, over and over again every day, to this very day. These days, he is not only talking but can walk unaided for over 100 meters and is living independently with occasional therapy support. His mobility will continue to improve in the years to come as he gains further strength and control of his leg muscles.

<u>Jay's Recovery Journey</u>:

Throughout this entire time, my son Jay kept improving during the 11 years spent under my guidance and support. It was not an easy road, regaining skills he had lost resulting from his Acquired Brain Injury, with many challenges faced along the way. For some time, Jay was not too wise in the company he chose to keep. It created difficulties, but that phase eventually passed. He completed a Certificate III qualification in Horticulture and began assisting me with running our youth camps and conducting our Bushwalks. Jay then went on to successfully complete a Diploma in Community Welfare & Counselling at Gold Coast TAFE, which eventually led to his employment as a youth worker.

For someone who was not a natural student, someone who was previously more interested in looking out of the classroom window at nature, this was a huge achievement.

Ben and Jay at Jay's TAFE Graduation

You may ask why I have not written more about Jay's recovery. Well, there is far more to Jay's and my complex journey together during those 11 years. But that is far too long a story for now and will be covered at greater length in my forthcoming book:

'Eleven Remarkable Years'

<u>New Beginnings</u>:

On my part, I'm still running my youth charity, New Beginnings International,[3] 25 years after having founded the non-profit organisation in 1999. Along the way, I have witnessed many successes, creating positive change in thousands of Queensland's most vulnerable children's lives.

Many of our past program participants have gone on to university, graduating in fields such as teaching and social work. Others have become leaders either at their school or within their communities. In one way or another, all of their lives have changed positively.

Ben Braeuer and Senior Self-esteem and Leadership Camp Participants

In recent years, we have had a new focus, successfully expanding the conservation part of our programs. In 2020, we created an entirely new Youth Marine Conservation Program that has been running successfully since then and has gained wide acclaim from all of the involved parties - students, parents, teachers, and school principals.

The latest addition to our charity's Marine Conservation program is a Reef Preservation Project, run in November 2024 in Australia's Whitsunday Islands, ably assisted by one of my former interns from the Gold Coast's Griffith University, Kim (since graduated as Marine Biologist), the other Marine Science intern Stephanie from Townsville's James Cook University. During the project, we conducted a series of Coral Surveys in Australia's Whitsunday Islands.

Coral Health Surveys using University of Queensland's 'Coral Watch' Coral Health Charts

© Copyright Bernd H-J H Braeuer December 2025

Whitsunday News NEWSPAPER

project

By **Deborah Friend**   *November 19, 2024*   💬 *0*

👁 *12*

Ben Brauer, Stephanie Cornish and Kimberly Wong about to set off on their first day of conducting coral surveys in several target sites in the Whitsunday Islands. Photo Deborah Friend.

The Lessons of 'Climbing Mountains, Reaching Goals':

Much of what follows was created spontaneously at the time of running my Self Awareness Group at Headway Gold Coast, based on my past life experience. With many of Headway's clients not able to see a future for themselves after their ABI diagnosis, they needed something to cling onto to give them new hope. This presentation was a simple way of getting them to confront and feel comfortable with the challenges that many of them would face. The diagrams included below are my originals (post-Laminex era), drawn again for later sessions at Headway's new premises on flip chart.

1. Stepping Out of The Box:

It takes 'Determination' to step 'Out of the box,' which either you or someone else may have placed you in. Far too often, others place restrictions on you for fear of insurance claims. Once you can see beyond the 'Invisible Walls' that have been placed around you, you can begin to visualise a more definite path forward.

2. Overcoming Challenges:

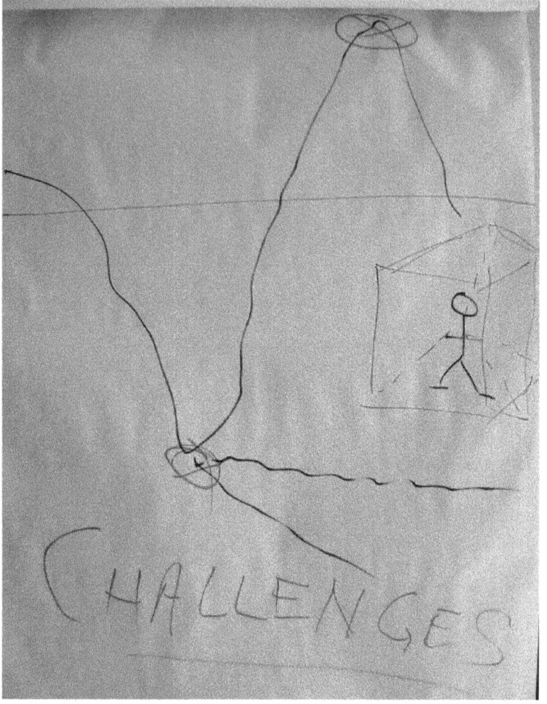

We are in that 'Box,' and we look at the seemingly huge challenges facing us. How will I ever be able to reach My Goal at the Top of that seemingly unconquerable Mountain? The old bit of wisdom that I learned as part of the Time Manager Course applies:

"How do you eat an Elephant? One small piece at a time!"

So, you learn to take your challenges, different in every case (especially if coping with an ABI), and divide them up into small and more manageable tasks. Then tackle them bit by bit!!

3. Trust Overcomes Fear:

There will be many challenges in Climbing 'your' Mountain, but if you take it in stages that match your ability, you can do it. It needs 'Trust' in your ability to build up slowly, and a good amount of 'Courage.' Some 'Loving Support' always helps. And very much, to take 'Measured Breaks along your Journey.' Those 'Huts' are there for a reason. At first, you may not be able to see the 'Top of the Mountain' with those 'Clouds Obscuring the View,' but as long as you keep mentally visualising reaching 'your' goal, whatever it may be, you'll make it. 'Take a Break' and 'Uncloud Your Vision,' especially after a strenuous part on 'Your Way to the Top'! Once you reach it, there is always the next goal to conquer waiting on the next mountain.

4. Overcoming Obstacles/Time out to Rest and Recover

There will be the inevitable obstacles that you will face when striving for 'your' goal at the Top of that Mountain. The trick is to be as prepared as possible before you embark on your challenge. Try to visualise in advance what you will need along the way. It might be practicing special skills like rock climbing, taking a course, or enlisting the help of friends. When you have overcome a particularly difficult obstacle along the way, take time out to rest, reflect, and recover before you move onto the next stage of the climb towards 'your' ultimate goal.

5. Achieving Your Dreams:

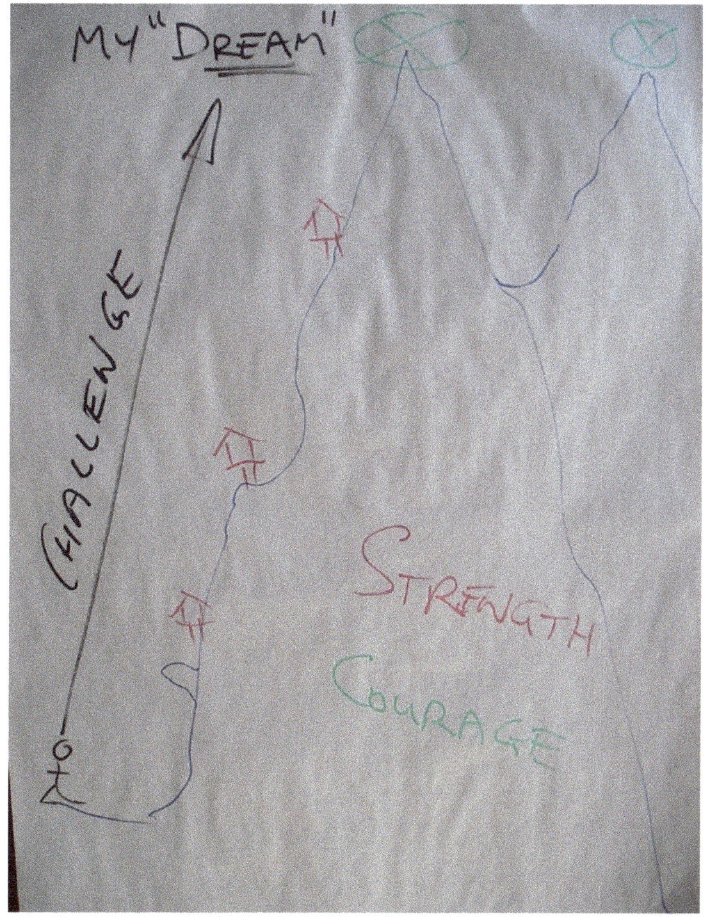

Make sure that that 'Dream' of yours becomes strong
enough in your own mind. 'Visualise it over and over
again' to build up the 'Strength' and 'Courage' you
need to take that 'First Step' – the most important one!
Once you do, with every subsequent step, that 'Dream'
will become more and more 'Real' and 'Achievable.'

Special NOTE: Taking Shortcuts doesn't help you:

There is one more drawing that I don't have anymore. During one of my sessions, one of the Headway clients commented, *"I'll just hire a Helicopter to reach the top of the mountain."*

I said, *"Sure, but you would miss all the experiences and the strengths you would have gained if you had actually taken on that 'Journey up your Mountain'!*

Climbing Mountains, Reaching Goals – Excerpts from Ben Braeuer's Life - Meeting the Challenges that Life presents you with:

Papua New Guinea - Our Equipment is missing

After spending a year learning the ropes as a Project Engineer at Ericsson working on the company's Colombo Plan (Indonesia) Project, my boss handed over sole market responsibility for Telecommunications Sales and Project Management in Papua New Guinea to me.

From the beginning, things progressed extremely well. I had already established a far more positive business relationship with Posts & Telegraphs PNG, and we had managed to win the latest round of contracts to expand Papua New Guinea's national Public Telecommunications Network, in the process also knocking out our company's two competitors.

It was now a critical time with projects under our new contracts about to begin. I needed to ensure that we got off to a great start. So, I booked my flight to Port Moresby to be there for the beginning of our new contracts. Equipment for the first telephone exchange expansions under our new contracts had already been shipped up from Melbourne by sea freight. I expected our PNG office manager to have everything under control.

The reality was quite the opposite. After I landed, I soon found out that the cases of equipment for our first job, an upgrade of the local telephone exchange at Popondetta village on the opposite side of the country, had been distributed over three separate stores located in widely separated parts of Port Moresby, mixed in with equipment for other jobs. Total confusion! What to do?

Well, it wouldn't do any good to panic. We had deadlines to meet. So, I got on the phone together with Ericsson's local office manager. In a short time, we had organised a driver, truck, and forklift. I hopped on board the truck with the driver, a grizzled-looking older local Papuan gent, who drove me to each of the three equipment stores in turn. I then managed to persuade the staff at each location to give us a hand. After a fair bit of sorting out and shuffling around cases, we had all the equipment for the Popondetta job on board. We drove into the Port Moresby Airport grounds with our equipment just as the sun was setting.

The next morning, I returned to the airport. After a short wait, an announcement came over the intercom, "Mr Braeuer, your charter flight is waiting!"

Well, the only way to get to Popondetta is by plane crossing over the Owen Stanley Range, the southeastern part of the central mountain chain in Papua New Guinea, with its highest point at 4,038 meters. The height at which DC-3s demonstrably begin to flap their wings.

What greeted me on the tarmac was a WWII vintage Douglas DC3. A very reliable aircraft, perfectly suited for this job. Mind you, my first ever flight in a DC3 years before was when the port engine caught fire as we were circling above Melbourne's old Essendon Airport! We survived that, making an emergency landing at Tullamarine airport on one engine!

Inside the plane, all of the seats had been removed, and our equipment cases had been solidly strapped down in the body of the plane.

After a friendly greeting, the co-pilot took me to the front of the plane and pointed me to the flop-down seat in the narrow passageway leading up to the cockpit.

It was an exciting flight to Popondetta, and after unloading the equipment, back again to Port Moresby. I ended up standing in the cockpit behind the pilot and co-pilot most of the way, spotting numerous hilltop mountain villages from high in the air as we made our way over the Owen Stanley's.

Most importantly, our equipment reached Popondetta on time for our technicians to begin the installation.

So now I ask you?

What would have happened if I had panicked and not accepted the challenge I was presented with when nothing was the way it should have been on my arrival in Port Moresby?

Well, our first project under the new contracts would have been delayed, losing face with our customer, PNG Posts and Telegraphs, and possibly risking penalties being awarded against our firm as a result.

Inaction always has consequences! In the case of climbing an actual mountain, we could get trapped in a blizzard and freeze to death!

… or in life, we simply fail to reach our dream goal!

Success can produce unexpected Rewards:

As a result of the work I did with our company's Papua New Guinea market, I was given the task to manage Ericsson's most important new Hi-tech project - Expansion of the Australian Public Telecommunications Network, introducing the latest Ericsson Technology into Australia.

Soon, I was leading Telecom Australia's technical staff on their first introductory Project Visit to Ericsson's headquarters in Stockholm to allow them to acquaint themselves with all aspects of introducing the new technology.

Greater details of my incredible Life Journey is part of a much longer story to be told in my other forthcoming book:

'The Boy Who Learned How to Fly"

The Ability to take that First Important Step:

I left the corporate world in 1991 in order to have more time to look after my two sons after becoming a sole parent, in the process becoming an independent consultant and also creating my own motivational course, 'Focus for Achievement.' I first ran the program for students at the Gold Coast TAFE College and also soon afterward for the crew of Sid Fisher and Australia's Americas Cup Yachting Challenger – Sydney 95.

Ben pictured with Sid Fisher's Sydney 95 Americas Cup
Challenge Team Members at Southport Yacht Club

During one of my Focus for Achievement TAFE classes, one
of the young women in the group approached me after my
second session. She confessed that she had difficulty with
the challenge I had given each of my students at the end of
the class - to do something they would never have dreamed
of doing by challenging themselves. She admitted that she
was far too shy to do anything like that!

We talked for a while after class, with me trying to open her
up further to the idea, focussing on what she would miss out
on in life if she kept avoiding challenging situations.
Afterward, I wondered if my words had had any effect at all.

When she arrived early for our next class a week later, she
couldn't wait to tell me about how she had dared to book

herself on a catamaran adventure cruise and how much she had enjoyed the experience. "I even did boom netting with water splashing all over me and I lost my bikini top, too, but I didn't care. I had so much fun!"

If you don't challenge yourself and take that first step into the unknown,

… nothing will change!

Time out is Essential:

I had learned about the 'Time out Principle' a long time ago. If you're caught up on a problem and don't seem to be getting anywhere, take time out, even if it's just as simple as a short walk or drive to a nearby shop.

I was in Munich for a month at Siemens Headquarters. I joined the company in 1980 in a new position as Sales and Project Manager after leaving Ericsson. During this time in Munich, I was working on a major business proposal with twenty or so Head Office sales and technical staff assisting me. We were on the 11th floor in the Siemens Telecommunications Building – the 'Hochhaus' (highest building on the southern side of Munich with an incredible view of the Alps from the higher floors). My then-boss and I, as well as Siemens regional manager for Australia and Indonesia, were debating a critical point in the preparations for this multi-million-dollar proposal. Despite our best efforts, we were not getting anywhere.

Suddenly, we spontaneously agreed and said, "Let's get out of here!" At the suggestion of one of Siemens' directors, we ended up at a restaurant located in a posh suburb on the southern side of Munich located at the 'Tennis club Grosshesselohe'. Over a delightful meal and drinks, we talked about anything but the problem we had been stuck on. After two-and-a-half relaxed hours, we were back at the office, and ….

The solution to the problem that we had been stuck on earlier … simply just presented itself.

The time away had cleared our minds and allowed us to think more freely than before when we had still been 'in the thick of it'!

Stepping out of the Box - Breaking Free of Constraints:

Shortly before the department I had been working in at Siemens was closed down, I was promoted to a special position working directly under the Australian and New Zealand regional Managing Director of global giant Siemens, Klaus Lahr. Based on the work I had already done in marketing and as one of three key members of the firm's 'Opportunity Team,' my brief in this special position was to seek out new opportunities for the firm. One of my tasks was to explore export opportunities, a difficult thing when you have Siemens companies or agencies in almost every country around the world, corporate policy forbidding Siemens companies from pursuing business in another Siemens company's territory.

It was time to break free of constraints and begin to think 'outside the box' that Siemens company policy had placed us in! My first step was to engage AUSTRADE – the Australian Trade Commission – in a special project designed to examine Siemens Australia's unique capabilities. One of the things that came out was that the Australia-based Siemens company had developed a unique Computer Software for Power Station Cabling.

Thinking outside the box, I came up with the dramatic concept that it would be better for Siemens globally if Siemens Australia won the tender for the new Bang Pakong Power Station (near Bangkok) … due to the significant advantage our Australian firm had with our special Power Station Cabling Software … rather than have the Thai Siemens company lose the tender against an outside competitor.

As a result, we formed an Australian Consortium, joining with Australian construction firm John Holland. We submitted our tender, and then had our General Manager of Electrical Engineering fly to Thailand to bless the project at a local temple even before the tender results were announced.

As a result, we won what was at the time Australia's largest-ever export order to Thailand for the Bank Pakong Power Station, a project valued then at around A$250 million, with Siemens taking responsibility for the electrical work and John Holland for the construction work.

It pays to think with a different mindset. Be creative!

Unblock yourself from the constraints that others put around you!

Setting Goals:

Focus on Things that bring New Meaning or New Experiences into Your Life:

It is easy to wish for things like making a million dollars, especially in today's society when so many think they can get rich without putting any real work in. Real opportunities are few and far between!

So, you should ask yourself:

- *Is the goal that I'm setting for myself achievable?*
- *What do I need to do to be able to achieve that goal?*
- *Do I have the strength to follow it through to the end?*

There is only one way that works – You must visualise your desired end result over and over again, just like Gerry did, **<u>until it becomes firmly imprinted in your mind</u>**.

I remember reading about an experiment that was performed with college students in America.

Students were divided into three groups:

- Group 1 practiced shooting basketball hoops over and over again, day after day.

- Group 2 did nothing.

- Group 3 simply visualised shooting baskets over and over again but did not physically practice shooting hoops at all.

When each group was tested at the end of the experiment, the result was something like this:

- Group 1 students made 85-95% of their shots.
- Group 2 only made 35-45% of their shots.

whilst,

- ***Group 3 made 80-90% of their shots, having only visualised doing so!***

THE POWER OF THE MIND IS INCREDIBLE!

Accepting Change and Moving with it:

I guess I've been the sort of person from a very young age who just takes things in his stride. Like the time my family's destiny was completely turned around while my parents and

I were having afternoon coffee in our first-floor apartment in one of my Oma's (grandmother's) two houses in my original home town northern Germany.

The year was 1960. Papa (Dad) was supposed to go by train to Bavaria in southern Germany later that afternoon to find accommodation for us. The carpentry/joinery he had been running for several years in my Opa's (grandfather's) old factory located directly behind Oma's main house had closed down, and Dad had been offered a job working as a machinist in a factory making ladies' stockings in a town just a little south of Munich in Bavaria.

The large envelope the postman brought that afternoon would change our family's and very much my own destiny in ways I could never possibly have imagined. Our family had been accepted as part of the Australian Post-War Immigration Program designed to attract skilled workers from Britain and European countries such as Italy, Greece, and Germany.

My parents had many reasons for applying to come to Australia. There were new opportunities, of course, but another main one was that my father had never wanted me to be involved in war. He had been lucky to survive WWII with his life after being wounded. If we had stayed in Germany, I would have been forced to complete two years of compulsory service in the German armed forces in my early twenties.

So instead of southern Germany, we soon found ourselves on a converted former German Freighter – the Cogedar

Line's M/V Aurelia - leaving Bremerhaven on a one-month voyage through the Mediterranean, picking up Italian migrants in Messina, Sicily, going on through the Suez Canal and then via the Indian Ocean to Australia, only narrowly skirting a Cyclone.

The day after we arrived in Melbourne, Australia, we were put on a train to the ex-army Migrant Camp at Bonegilla near the Victoria/New South Wales border.

For me, the whole trip halfway around the world was simply one big adventure. I took it in my stride - except for the sea sickness that both my parents and I had to suffer through.

One day, as we were passing through the edge of the storm, I remember standing outside of the ship's main saloon doors with my mum and other passengers. Not far from the railing, huge waves swept past. When I think of it now, if a massively large wave had come past, every single one of us would have been swept overboard. It never worried me at the time.

I did not realise at the time how much this inbuilt ability to remain calm would assist me during real crises later in life!

The ability to accept change and run with it is a real strength to have in your life!

Faced with Disaster – Fight or Flight:

We had become very settled to life in our new country, Australia. It was 1969. Apollo 11 had just made its successful Moon landing. I skipped my afternoon engineering class to drive home in my VW Beetle to watch the grainy black and white live broadcast of Neil Armstrong descending the Lunar Lander's ladder to utter those historic words, "That's one small step for man. One giant leap for mankind."

My dad loved watching boxing on late-night TV. I had already gone to bed and was almost asleep in my room when my mum's tearful voice intruded, begging me for help.

What I found was my dad lying on the floor, not moving, not breathing. What could I do? I'd never been taught first aid but had seen people doing mouth-to-mouth resuscitation on TV. So, I got down on my knees and tried to replicate what I had seen them do. To this day, I still carry the memory of the taste of the Vaseline my dad used to smear on his lips to stop them from cracking.

After some time with no response, I gave up and literally ran to the public phone box on our street corner and called our family doctor. It was already after 11 at night. He asked me to describe the situation and then told me to that all I could do was to ring an ambulance. After I got home, Mum and I tried to move dad. He was not a light man. Mum was in total despair.

Distraught, I sat down on our lounge. I remember breaking down and crying for half an hour or more. Then, just as suddenly, the tears dried up. I realised that I had to face the fact that my mum was not coping. There was only one thing for me to do. I pulled out the metal lock box that Dad kept all his important papers in and started looking through them to see what we were facing.

My answer was to stay and fight rather than take flight!

To make matters worse, Mum, within weeks of Dad's death, lost both her mother and sister in Germany. She subsequently broke down completely for an extended period of time.

Over the coming months, at age 19, I was managing my mum's breakdown and also faced the task of fighting off our mortgagors so we could remain in our home. All of this whilst finishing off the last year and a half of my engineering studies.

Well, we did manage to keep our house, and I finally graduated my studies as an Electronics Engineer.

I dare not think what would have happened if I had not remained strong when it was needed the most.

One of my favourite poems has always been Rudyard Kipling's 'If.' The first part goes like this:

"If you can keep your head when all about you are losing theirs ..."

If you can remain strong in a time of crisis, it prepares you to achieve just about anything. You will gain the ability to overcome the toughest challenges!

Additional Books to be published by Ben Braeuer in 2025/26:

'Eleven Remarkable Years – Managing my Son's Brain Injury Recovery and creating our Youth Charity'

'The Boy who learned how to Fly – How a move to Australia allowed a 10-year-old German Boy to become a champion at the highest level of International Business'

© Copyright Bernd H-J H Braeuer December 2025

References:

[1] **Headway Gold Coast** Inc. is a charitable organisation supporting people in the community who have suffered an Acquired Brain Injury (ABI)

[2] A Frenchman named Emile Coué originally coined the potentially life-changing phrase around a century ago.

[3] **New Beginnings International Association Inc.** (founded 1999) is an Australian ACNC registered Youth Charity - Early Age Intervention programs for vulnerable and at-risk children and young people and Marine Conservation Programs. Recognised for innovation in youth prevention (Sweden 2010). Finalist in the 2017 Telstra Business Awards (charities category).

Website: https://www.newbeginningsinternational.com

Facebook: https://www.facebook.com/New-Beginnings-109219429192591

Instagram & LinkedIn: New Beginnings International

New Beginnings International – Youth Self-esteem and Leadership Programs & Camps

Citation:

Bernd (Ben) Braeuer is a former international corporate executive, most recently holding responsibility for corporate strategy (Australia, New Zealand and Asia-Pacific) at global giant Siemens before choosing to step away from the company in 1991 for family reasons. He holds the following formal and supplementary study qualifications:

- Dip. Electronic Engineering – PIT/RMIT University
- Graduate Marketing – Australian Institute of Management (AIM)
- Siemens Corporate Training (Australia & Germany)
- Asia/Pacific Regional Studies & Business Council Memberships (Australia/Papua New Guinea, Australia/Malaysia)
- Train-the-Trainer – Gold Coast TAFE
- Certificate IV in Workplace Assessment & Training

- Yachting Instructor/Yachtmaster Offshore
- Natural Healing Methodologies, Yoga, Tai-Chi, Indigenous Cultures & Communities
- Studies in Globalisation & World Economics
- Academic Writing - Griffith University
- Swedish Social System - Stockholm University

During Ben's corporate years, he:

- Managed Ericsson's Colombo Plan Project – Indonesia
- Managed Ericsson's Papua New Guinea Business through Independence, developing new business opportunities and creating a solid ongoing corporate relationship
- Managed the introduction of the latest Ericsson Digital Technology into Australia's Public Telecommunications Network
- Managed introduction and marketing of Siemens latest Digital Technology into Australia's Private Telecommunications Networks
- Led Siemens 'Opportunity Team' and was subsequently given responsibility for Corporate Strategy (Australia, New Zealand and Asia Pacific Region) in a special position with direct responsibility to the firm's Managing Director
- Had direct responsibility for University and Technology Cooperations; Export Strategy leading to the largest ever order in Thailand by an Australian Consortium; General Corporate Strategy putting together the ten-year forward strategy for the firm

Awards of Excellence:

**Ben Braeuer – New Beginnings - Finalist in the 2017
Telstra Business Awards (Charities Category)**

Book Overview:

If you're looking for a book that's equal parts inspiring, heartfelt, and practical, *Climbing Mountains, Reaching Goals* by Bernd Braeuer (or Ben, as he prefers to be called) definitely makes it up that list. This memoir is more than just a self-help book; it's a deeply personal journey between Ben's own life experiences and the sheer willpower it takes to overcome and heal through a traumatic event.

The book immediately starts off with a gut-wrenching moment that sets the tone for the entire narrative: Ben's son, Jay, suffers a heart stoppage that leaves him with an Acquired Brain Injury (ABI). What follows is a father's emotional and physical struggle as he comes to terms with his new reality, determined to make his efforts worthwhile. The story extends beyond recovery and shows how Ben turned this tragedy into a mission to help others facing similar challenges.

Drawing from his experiences in the corporate world, becoming a motivational coach, yoga instructor, and founder of a youth charity, Ben is able to develop a program called *Climbing Mountains, Reaching Goals*, which becomes the backbone of this book. The program is designed to help people suffering from similar injuries, dealing with personal setbacks, or just trying to achieve their dreams—break free from the "boxes" they've been placed in and climb their own metaphorical mountains.

The book is filled with personal anecdotes that are both touching and relatable. From his son's recovery to his work with Headway Gold Coast, Ben shares stories of real people who've defied the odds. Gerry's story, in particular, is truly inspiring: a man who had been told he'd never walk or talk again after brain surgery.

While minding the balance between emotional and practical, Ben doesn't just tell you to "climb the mountain"; he gives you a step-by-step guide on how to do it. He breaks down the process into manageable steps, sometimes aided by his hand-drawn diagrams, adding a charming personal touch to the book.

Author's Website:

https://www.berndbrauer.com